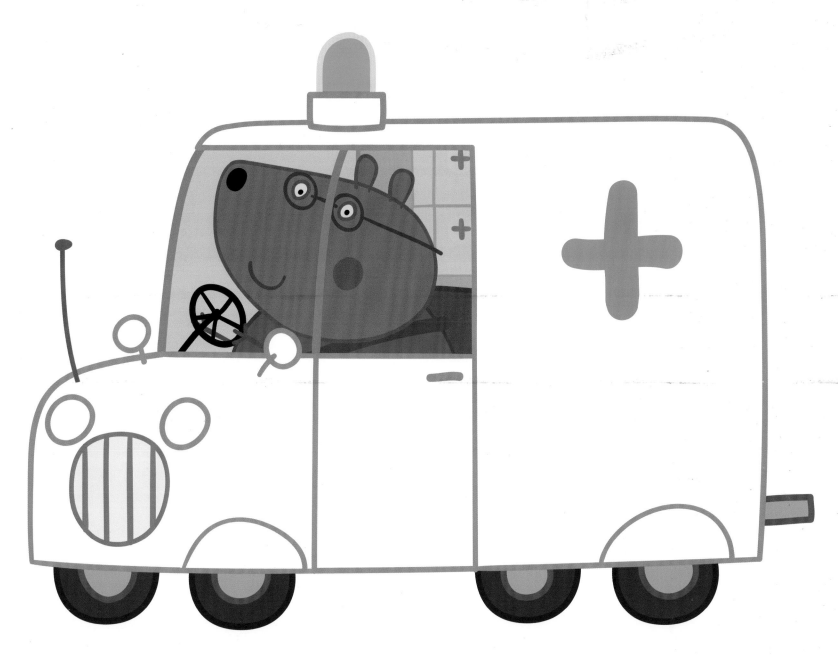

This book belongs to

LADYBIRD BOOKS

UK | USA | Canada | Ireland | Australia | India | New Zealand | South Africa

Ladybird Books is part of the Penguin Random House group of companies
whose addresses can be found at global.penguinrandomhouse.com.

www.penguin.co.uk   www.puffin.co.uk   www.ladybird.co.uk

Penguin
Random House
UK

First published 2020
001

Printed in the United Kingdom by Print 4 Limited

A CIP catalogue record for this book is available from the British Library

ISBN: 978-0-241-48069-4

All correspondence to:
Ladybird Books
Penguin Random House Children's
One Embassy Gardens,
8 Viaduct Gardens, London SW11 7BW

Peppa Loves Doctors and Nurses

It was People Who Help Us Day at playgroup, and everyone was excited.
"Now, children," began Madame Gazelle, "today we have two very special visitors. They are both people who help us!"

"Is one the Queen?" asked Peppa.
"Is one my aunty?" asked Rebecca Rabbit.
"Dine-saw ROAR?" asked George.

"Three wonderful guesses," said Madame Gazelle.
"But the people coming to see us today are
Dr Brown Bear and Nurse Fox!"

"Hooray!" cheered the children, jumping up and down.
They **loved** Dr Brown Bear and Nurse Fox.

"When I hurt my leg, I had to go to hospital," said Pedro Pony.
"Dr Brown Bear and Nurse Fox looked after me."

"When I was feeling poorly," said Peppa,
"Dr Brown Bear made me all better."

Just then, there was
a noise from outside.
The children ran to
the window to look.

"Madame Gazelle!
It's Dr Brown Bear
and Nurse Fox!"

"Good morning, everyone," said Dr Brown Bear. "Today, Nurse Fox and I are going to talk to you about keeping fit and staying healthy! Let's start by going over to the playground and getting our bodies moving."

"Yippee!" cheered the children.
They loved moving around outside.

Dr Brown Bear and Nurse Fox had built an obstacle course.
"To keep fit and healthy, we must move our bodies every day," said Dr Brown Bear.
"Madame Gazelle will show us all how it's done."

The children watched in amazement as Madame Gazelle completed the obstacle course perfectly. "Ta-da!" she cried.

"Now it's your turn, children," said Dr Brown Bear.
"Ready . . . Steady . . . GO!"
Peppa and her friends set off.

They swung . . .

crawled . . .

hopped . . .

slid . . .

skipped . . .

and jumped around.

"This is so much fun, isn't it, Suzy?" cheered Peppa. But, as she turned to Suzy Sheep, Peppa forgot to look where she was going, and . . .

... fell on her bottom.
"Oops!" cried Peppa.

THUMP!

Nurse Fox came straight over. "Are you all right?" she asked.
"I think so," said Peppa.
"Good," said Nurse Fox, checking that Peppa was not hurt.
"You can carry on now, Peppa, but please be careful!"
"Thank you for helping me!" said Peppa.

Peppa loved the obstacle course.
"This is my **favourite** bit!"
she cried, jumping high and landing
in a big muddy puddle.
"I'm not sure that's part of the course,
Peppa," said Madame Gazelle, smiling.

SPLASH!

"Snack time!" called Nurse Fox.
"Hooray!" cheered the children.
"Don't forget to wash your hands before
you eat," said Nurse Fox.

All the children went to wash their hands.
Peppa and Rebecca sang the "Wash Your Hands" song . . .

"Wash, wash, wash our hands,
Wash them nice and clean!
Bubbly scrubbly, scrubbly bubbly!
Wash them nice and clean!"

"Eating healthy food helps us stay fit and strong,"
said Dr Brown Bear as he tried to open his snack box.
"Hmm. This seems to be stuck. Er, Nurse Fox, could
you help me, please?"

Nurse Fox came over and opened the box easily.
"Nurse Fox," gasped Peppa, "you must eat lots of
healthy food to be that strong!"
Everyone laughed.

Peppa and her friends loved snack time.
"Yummy!" they cried.
Keeping fit and strong was delicious!

"You've done such a good job today, children," said Dr Brown Bear when they'd finished. "I'm going to give you all a sticker!"
"Hooray!" cheered the children. They loved stickers, too!

Madame Gazelle brought out the dressing-up box. "It's time for you to be the doctors and nurses now, children," she said. Peppa and her friends had lots of fun dressing up.

"Dr Brown Bear," said Peppa the Doctor,
"you must keep fit and stay healthy, too!"
"Of course!" he replied.

The children took Dr Brown Bear outside and told him to go around and around the obstacle course.

"One more time!"
cried Peppa the Doctor.
"OK . . . *puff* . . . How's . . . *puff* . . . this?"
gasped Dr Brown Bear.

When he was allowed to stop, he looked quite tired.
"Dr Brown Bear doesn't look very well," said Peppa the Doctor.
"I think he needs a plaster!"

"And bandages," added Nurse Danny Dog.
"And more bandages!" added Nurse Suzy.
"Now he needs a sticker," said Peppa the Doctor.
All the little doctors and nurses covered Dr Brown Bear in stickers.

"Thank you for being so helpful," said Dr Brown Bear.
He was covered in so many bandages, he couldn't move.
What a *patient* patient he was!

"What do we say to our visitors?" asked Madame Gazelle.
"Thank you, Dr Brown Bear! Thank you, Nurse Fox!"
cheered the children, giving them a big clap!

CLAP! CLAP! CLAP!

Peppa loves doctors and nurses.
Everyone loves doctors and nurses!